GAY ERO

ADVENTURES
AT THE LAKE

Dick Clinton

CW00918674

WARNING

This book contains sexually explicit scenes and adult language. It may be considered offensive to some readers. This book is for sale to adults ONLY.

* * * * * * * * * * * * * * * * * * *

Please store your files wisely where they cannot be accessed by underage readers.

Please feel free to send me an email. Just know that these emails are filtered by my publisher. Good news is always welcome.

Dick Clinton - **dick_clinton@awesomeauthors.org**

Copyright © 2013 by Dick Clinton

All Rights reserved under International and Pan-American Copyright Conventions. By payment of required fees you have been granted the non-exclusive, non-transferable right to access and read the text of this book. No part of this text may be reproduced, transmitted, downloaded, decompiled, reverse-engineered or stored in or introduced into any information storage and retrieval system, in any form or by any means, whether electronic or mechanical, now known, hereinafter invented, without express written permission of BLVNP Inc. For more information contact BLVNP Inc. The publisher does not have any control over and does not assume any responsibility for author or third-party websites or their content. This book is a work of fiction. The characters, incidents and dialogue are drawn from the author's imagination and are not to be construed as real. While reference might be made to actual historical events or existing locations, the names, characters, places and incidents are either products of the author's imagination or are used fictitiously, and any resemblance to actual persons living or dead, business establishments, events or locales is entirely coincidental.

About the Publisher

BLVNP Incorporated, A Nevada Corporation, 340 S. Lemon #6200, Walnut CA 91789, info@blvnp.com / legal@blvnp.com

NOTE: Due to the highly emotional reaction of some people to works of erotic fiction, any email sent to the above address that contains foul language or religious references is automatically deleted by our anti-spam software and will not be seen. All other communications are welcome.

DISCLAIMER

Please don't be stupid and kill yourself. This book is a work of FICTION. Do not try any new sexual practice that you find in this book. It is fiction and not to be confused with reality. Neither the author nor the publisher or its associates assume any responsibility for any loss, injury, death or legal consequences resulting from acting on the contents in this book. Every character in this book is over 18 years of age. The author's opinions are not to be construed as the opinions of the publisher. The material in this book is for entertainment purposes ONLY. Enjoy.

Adventures at the Lake
Gay Erotica

By: Dick Clinton

© Dick Clinton 2014
ISBN: 978-1-62761-715-4

Arrival at the Lake Cabin

Roy Jordan, the young man at the drive in theater, asked me to join him and two of his school buddies at his parent's cabin at Olathe Lake for the week-end. Roy and his father ran the projectors at the drive in theater. I had met Roy during my intimate sexual encounters with two of the Security Men in the Employees restroom. This is where I first lost my virginity and shared my ass with Roy. He seemed to like me and offered me a ride home that evening. We pulled onto a dark road and two brothers from a local farm forced us to participate in a hot and sexy encounter. Roy did things he'd never done before with men and he swore me to secrecy. Because of this secret, we had a special bond.

Even though I was in my senior year in high school and still living at home, I had to get permission to go to the cabin with Roy and his friends. They assumed I would not drink or take drugs and I was a good boy. Humph. If they only knew how good I was to and with my buddies. I gave Roy a call and told him I could go with them and he was to pick me up Saturday.

Early Saturday morning Roy and the other guys pulled up in front of my house in a small van and we were on our way to the lake. It was only about 15 miles from my house and would only take us a short time to get there. The guys wanted to stop by a Short-Stop and pick up some beer and a few other snacks to add to the other food item. You know how young teenagers are about eating.

I was introduced to the two guys, Jason and Chad that attended Roy's Junior College. Jason was a tall clean cut looking guy with nice tan, sandy blond hair, pleasant smile, a great set of teeth, and had an athletic lanky swimmers body. He didn't show much of a bulge in his cut-offs but sometimes a tall guy can surprise you because it hangs down his leg instead of stuffed in his crotch area.

Chad was shorter than Jason and Roy, but about the same height as I. He was solid in stature, had dark curly hair, and a square jaw, with a small crevice in his chin. He seemed a bit shy, but showed a nice bulge under his shorts. I pictured him to have a thick cock and golf ball size hairy balls. I notice a few hairs protruding from his 'wife beater' shirt and soft fuzzy hair on his solid firm legs. I figured him to be either a wrestler or a jogger by the way he moved.

We were soon on our way and would arrive at the lake soon. It had been a nice calm sunny day and the lake looked calm and good for boating or water skiing. Soon as we arrived at the cabin everyone grabbed something to unload the van.

The cabin was small but large enough to accommodate the four of us guys. It had a small screened in porch in front. Inside the cabin was one large room with two couches that made into beds, couple small end tables with lamps and a small fireplace with butane burning fake logs. To the left of the room was a small bedroom area with a double bed. You had to go thru the bedroom to enter the small toilet, sink, and shower. In back of the main room was a small kitchen with a counter and bar stools. Behind the back of the kitchen was a large screened in porch with several lounge chairs and small dining table, refrigerator and a couch large enough for a person to sleep on.

Roy and I would sleep in the bedroom and Jason and Chad were to sleep on the couch/beds in the living area. It was nothing fancy but clean. I expected no more than a family cabin. Jason and Chad had been here before and immediately took their swimming things to the dock. Jason and Roy went to the boathouse to check on the boat to see if it had gasoline and was in running condition. Chad and I unloaded the groceries and supplies and had a chance to set on the back porch and relax while the guys were at the boathouse. We sat there only briefly when Chad opened up and asked me about my personal sex life.

"Roy tells me you like guys and you're a great cocksucker. Is that correct or was he just kidding me?"

"Yeah. I like guys, and you have to judge for yourself about my cock sucking procedures"

"That's cool. I've never had a blow job from a guy before. Roy said you give better head than his girlfriends, because a guy knows how another guy likes to have it done. That makes sense."

I notice Chad was beginning to rearrange himself and started to move around in his chair.

"Yeah. I think a guy knows how another guy likes to make it feel. Would you like for me to show you? The guys seem to be occupied at the boathouse."

"Awe...I wasn't hinting for a blow job, but to be truthfully with you, I got a boner just thinking about it. You know me and Jason are not gay so don't expect me to precipitate."

"I know you guys aren't gay. That doesn't matter to me, in fact, I prefer servicing straight guys. I just like it that way, but later on I will show you some other ways I can satisfy you that you might enjoy just as much, if not better than just getting sucked off. Are you still in the mood for me to suck your cock?" I said as I moved over to Chad as he set on one of the lounge chairs.

"Ah, Ah. Sure. If you still want to. I can see the boathouse from here and if they come up the path we can stop."

I told Chad to stand as I pulled off his trunks. His cock was already starting to grow. I was a pretty good judge of cock size and I was correct. His cock was partially cut, thick and about six to seven inches long soft. His balls and pubic hair were covered with thick and dark hair.

He set back down on the chair as I moved between his hairy legs. He closed his eyes as I first caressed his balls and guided his fat cock to my lips. As his cock got harder the foreskin eased away from his tulip shaped cock head. Small amount of pre-cum was starting to form at the slit. I first licked the sweet nectar it offered then ran my tongue around his cock head a couple of times, and went all the way down on him with one quick movement. He sighed out.

"Oh my, gawd. Oh my gawd. That is fantastic. You took my whole cock. Yeah. Keep going, keep going. I love it."

I didn't need any encouragement and went back down on him over and over again. As I held on to his hairy balls, I slid my finger past his perineum to the tip of his anus. I kissed his cock up and down between breaths, then engulfed his cock over and over until I knew he was about to pop his load. He grabbed the back of my head and let out a moan of sexual pleasure and started to cum. I held on tight as he pushed his groin up to meet my cock sucking mouth. Then he moaned again and continued to cum.

I finished savoring his sweet load and licked his balls and cock clean and dry. He continued to set on the lounge and fell asleep. His swimming suit was on the floor and he remained naked. I was not about to wake this cute guy with the hairy body and fat dick. I wanted Roy and Jason to know I had just drained him of his first load.

I went back to the kitchen area and continued to put the food items away. I heard Roy and Jason talking as they came up the path to the cabin. Chad still remained asleep on the lounge chair. They came up the back stairs and onto the back porch. They didn't bother to wake Chad but went straight to the 'frig' to get a beer. Roy came into the kitchen and gave me a silly grin and hit me on the shoulder.

"I see you've broken in one of our guest already. I guess he must have enjoyed it because he's asleep. You next conquest will be Jason. We were talking about you when we were at the boathouse. He's interested."

Roy stood close to me as we talked. He pushed his warm body next to mine. He already had a hard on. I smiled at him and pulled down his trunks, got on my knees on the kitchen floor, took his cock in my mouth and started giving him a blow job. He remained standing drinking his beer and enjoying my mouth working over his hard throbbing cock. Jason came thru the area, saw our action, and went to the toilet to take a piss.

"Damn it Dick. I've missed your warm mouth on my hard cock. I jacked off every day thinking how nice you treated me. I'm anxious to fuck that sweet, tight ass again soon. But, man, this blow job is a well needed relief. Oh man. I'm gonna cum already. Are you ready? Here it comes. Here it comes. Oh damn that's so good. Uh huh. Mu-mm." Roy continued to gasp and enjoy his quick orgasm.

We finished our session, but I noticed Jason was still in the bathroom. I didn't want him to feel left out so I went to the bedroom. Jason was still standing at the toilet stool with a big hard on. He didn't look up when I came into the toilet. His trunks were down around his ankles. I just walked in, took hold of his big hard cock, dropped to my knees, and licked his cock head.

His cock was large, just like I'd guessed, and much larger than the other guys, and perfectly shaped. I was looking forward to getting fucked by this one, but one thing at a time. I wanted to taste his cock. He turned towards me and let me work on his cock. It was very thick and about ten inches in length.

I did the best I could at sucking him but thought I'd suggest that he fuck me. I motioned for him to follow me to the bed. I found some lube on the end table and after getting him as wet as I could, I rubbed some lube on his cock head. I stood, dropped my trunks and bent over the bed offering him my ass hole to fuck.

Jason softly said to me. "Are you sure you're up to this? No one has taken my cock all the way. I'll be gentle."

He rubbed his wet cock up and down my ass crack until he located my opening. He eased his cock head into my anus. He paused as it slowly eased directly into my body. Gawd, it was big, but I wanted it.

Just then he shoved it to the hilt. I felt his balls rest against my ass. I had him all the way in. I looked towards the open bedroom door and Roy was standing there jacking off again. He gave us a thumbs-p.

"You feel good in me Jason. After I get use to you cock, you can plow me as hard as you want. I like rough manly sex. Fuck me, Jason. Just fuck me good and shoot your hot cum in my ass."

"Fuck yeah. I'm glad you like it because I can fuck for a long time and can cum two or three times without pulling out. You sure you're ready for a hard fucking?"

Roy eased his way into the room and stood beside Jason as he started fucking me.

"I told you he was a willing fuck. Take your time and enjoy it. He loves it. I'll just watch for now, if you guys don't mind. It's amazing how he can take your big thick ten inch cock, but I did see him get fucked by a couple of the security guys at the Drive in theater. One of the guys has at least eleven inches. Man that's hot. Go for it Jason and I'll just stand here and enjoy if you don't mind."

"Fuck. I don't mind. I like to be watched but I never get the chance to fuck like this. I really appreciate you sharing your pussy-boy. This is amazing how easy he takes my cock so easy and it feels awesome. This is gonna be a great weekend. Oh yeah. Let me enjoy this ass. Uh huh." Jason said as he plowed my ass.

I saw Chad coming into the room. He didn't stop but went directly to the toilet. He was still naked. Jason continued to fuck me slow and easy, pulling his ten inches almost all the way out, then shoving it back in. Roy placed his hand on my buttocks then down to my hole to feel Jason's cock entering my asshole.

"Get him on the bed and turn him over on his back. He likes it better that way." Roy suggested to Jason.

Jason pulled out of my ass as I positioned myself on the bed. He quickly got on the bed with me, lifted my legs, put them on his shoulders, and tried to guide his cock into my ass again.

"Roy. Do us a favor. Guide my cock to his asshole before we fuck again. I don't want to injury him. You're not afraid to touch my dick are you?"

Roy got on the bed with us and took hold of Jason's cock and guided it to my wet hole. Jason braced his arms on the bed, looked down at me and winked. Meanwhile Chad had finished pissing in the toilet and was now watching the action on the bed. His cock was hard and ready for more action as well.

"Hey guys. Looks like we just might spend more time in bed than on the water. Gawd Jason! I didn't know your cock was so big. How the 'hell' does Dick take that big sausage? Don't stretch him out of shape. I've never fuck a dude's ass before. It looks as hot as any pussy. Save me some."

"There's plenty to go around. He loves to get fuck. You can go next if Jason ever gets his nuts. I've seen this dude fuck before and he can cum a couple times before he finished."

"Fuck. I don't know if I can hold off that long. He sucked me off while you guys were at the boathouse and it was great, but fucking really looks good too. I'll just wait and watch Jason at play. Hey, you want to go with me to get a beer and let these two fuck for a while?"

"Yeah. That might be best. If I stand here and watch this action very long, I'll pop my load again and I'm anxious to fuck."

Roy and Chad went into the other room to get a beer while Jason fucked me. He was a great fucker. He kept touching my prostate and I knew I could cum quickly but tried to hold back. Jason lifted my ass higher and plunged deeper.

"Damn. I never knew fucking ass could be so great. When I fuck the girls they say I'm hurting them and it turns me off and I hate using a condom. It kills all the feeling. I don't have to worry about getting you knocked up. Your ass is so warm and smooth. This is the best ever. I'm gonna shoot my first load soon so hang on, man, I'm going into action mode. Un huh. This is so good. Un, Un, Un. Oh fuck. Here comes my first load. Can I cum in you? Oh fuck. Too late. I'm cumming, I'm cumming. Oh gawd. Oh, Oh, Oh man"

Jason kept plunging his big cock into me as he came. He spread my legs and buried his cock deep and let it cum. I shot my first load with him. My cum shot all over my abs and chest. The expression on his face was awesome. He closed his eyes and smiled with pleasure and paused. He finally opened his eyes and looked down at me and smiled.

"That was unbelievable. I think I shot 6 or 8 times before I stopped cumming. I know my nuts needed draining but your ass made it feel so hot. I can cum again it you don't mind. Let my cock soak in your warm hole then I'll start fucking you again. You okay? I noticed you came so I did something right. Huh?"

Jason placed my legs back on his shoulders and rubbed his hand thru the cum on my abs, then he put his hand to my mouth for me to taste. I licked his fingers clean. He scooped up some more and put it to his mouth.

"Humm. Nice. Never tasted another guys cum before. Not bad. Not bad at all. It tastes like sweet cream."

He started to move in and out of my cum filled hole again. His cock was still hard for fucking. Once again we fucked me but a bit harder and longer this time. He gave me another good fucking and came in me again.

"That was as good as the first fuck. I'm being selfish. I should let the other guys pop their nuts now. What do you say? But don't get me wrong, I want a few more fuck from you later. Okay?" Then he called out to Roy.

"Hey Roy. If you'll bring us a beer I give you back your hot boy pussy, but just for a while. This is good stuff, I mean really good stuff."

Roy came into the room just as Jason was pulling his cum coated cock from my well fucked hole.

"Here's you beer. Put your cock up to his mouth and he'll clean it off for you, and while he's cleaning that cock for you, I'll put my cock in his ass for another good fucking. "

Jason moved up to my face as I started licking and cleaning his semi-hard cock and low hanging balls. Roy was getting hot watching his buddy's cock being serviced just a few inches from his face. Roy lifted my legs and buried his cock deep in my wet hole. I sighed at his sudden entry. Even though Roy's cock wasn't as big as Jason's it was curved differently and hit different spots. I liked being fucked by Roy.

I continued to clean Jason's ten inch cock while getting fucked by Roy. Jason was already starting to get hard again. Chad came back into the room to eagerly wait his turn at his first piece of male ass.

I motioned for him to get on the bed and put his cock in my mouth while I was still holding onto Jason's cock. Now I had the three hot guys on the bed with me. I alternated sucking on Jason, then Chad while Roy fucked me fast and hard.

Roy had already cum earlier when I sucked him off in the kitchen but he was ready to unload again in my ass. He started moaning and telling me he was gonna cum. I eagerly waited for his cum to be shot up my ass, when Jason started to shoot another load all over my face and into the corners of my mouth. He had another big load for me to savor.

I wanted Chad to fuck me so I held his cock tight so he would not cum yet. As soon as Roy pulled out of me, Chad mounted me and put his cock in my overflowing cum filled hole. He was so excited he only pumped me six times before he came. It was quick but nice. When he finished cumming he lay across my wet cum soaked body and licked some of Jason's cum from my face, then he lightly kissed my lips and turned his face away. I thought he was going to fall asleep again.

Jason and Roy collapsed on the bed with me and Chad. After a few minutes Roy got up and said we should check out the water and take a quick swim. Jason was the next to move, then Chad slowly got up and joined the other boys. I wanted to lay there and rest. I turned over on my stomach and fell asleep.

Who's touching my butt?

I don't know how long I'd been asleep but when I woke up someone was feeling my ass and running their hand up and down my wet hole. I spread my legs and was ready for another fucking. To my pleasant surprise I felt a warm breath on my ass and a finger sliding into my hole. Then the warm breath moved closer to my spreading ass crack.

Someone was spreading my ass and starting to rim me and sucking out the four loads of cum buried in my hot well fucked hole. His tongue felt good. His rough unshaven face was familiar. I dared to look over my shoulder and to my surprise it was Roy's dad, the projectionist at the Drive in Theater, eating my cum filled hole. This was the same person that ate me out when I was at the Drive in Theater and had gotten fucked several times that evening. I lay there not knowing what to do or say next, besides he was an excellent ass rimmer. I thought to myself what if his son Roy and Jason and Chad would come in. Boy would that be awkward. I started to get up, but Roy's dad kept on licking and sucking on my ass.

"Sir. I'm afraid the guys will be back soon and I don't think you want us to be caught in this position, do you?"

"I saw the boys leave a few minutes ago in the boat and they don't know I'm here. I knew you were gonna let the boys fuck you and I wanted to eat out your slutty boy-pussy again. I love to eat pussy but your ass full of hot young men's cum is even better. How many loads of cum are in you right now? You're nice and juicy. Please don't tell Roy and the boys I was here. Let me lick your ass some more then I'll jack off and leave before they get back. Please."

"Mr. Jordan, Sir. You can eat my ass all you want but why don't you add your cum to my pussy by giving me a good fucking and add your cum. I think that's hot. Just give me a good fucking like Roy does."

"That would be fantastic. You sure you wouldn't mind if I fuck you? I'm not a young stud like the boys but my cock is big and thick."

"Oh sir. I think you're kind of hot and by the looks of your big dick, I think I would enjoy having you fuck me. Just take off your pants and crawl on. I'm still nice and wet so you shouldn't have much trouble getting your cock in my ass. Please fuck me sir. I'd like that."

He got up from the bed and quickly took off his pants. I lay on my stomach and braced myself for another fuck. He was so nervous he was shaking but he managed to guide his cock to my wet hole and enter me. Wow. I was now gonna be fucked by father and son on the same day. This was gonna be a first for me.

He mounted me and put his thick cock up my ass. Even though I had been fucked four time today, his cock felt nice. He parted my buttock and watched his dick going in and out of my hole. I could feel his warm balls touching my balls. He fucked slow and easy but was so hot he started to cum after a few minutes. He gasped and moaned and stopped moving as he emptied his gushing load in my ass. He paused for a few minutes then pulled his spent cock out of my hole. He leaned forward and kissed each of my buttocks and quickly put his pants and shoes back on, patted my butt, and headed out the door.

The Welcome Intrusion

I started to get up and go to the toilet when I heard a sound in the other room. I assumed it was one or all of the guys that had returned from the boating. I went to the head, pissed and cleaned myself and returned to the bed room.

I was shocked to see a lake security guard standing in the doorway of the bedroom.

"Are you alright, son? I saw that man hurrying out the door and thought I would check the place out. I didn't know anyone was using the cabin this weekend. Who are you? Are you a guest of Roy and his family?

I was stunned seeing this stranger in the Cabin. I stood completely naked while standing before me, was a hot looking young stud about 25, dressed in a brown tailored security uniform. He was about six foot tall and solidly built. His blond hair edged from his uniform cap and his blue eyes sparkled as he slowly looked me up and down. I noticed a thick wedding band on his finger. I was starting to get excited and my dick started to get hard.

"Yes sir. I'm a guest of Roy Jordan. We'll be here for the week end. And who are you?"

"I'm Adam, the lake security officer. I keep watch of anything strange happening around here and by the looks of things, something strange just happened. That man sure rushed out of here for some reason. Were you the reason?"

"Yes officer I guess I'm the guilty one. Won't you come in the bedroom while I find some clothes to put on, unless you want to join me and get naked too." I brazenly utter to this hot looking officer. I notice a large bulge developing under his tailored uniform.

"I guess I could stay for a while. What did you have in mind?" he said as he moved closer to me.

As we talked my dick was at full mast and starting to ooze pre-cum juices. I got closer to him and rubbed his growing cock area. He started un-buckling his belt. He dropped his holster and nightstick to the floor as I dropped to my knees to unzip his uniform pants. As he pulled down his pants out jumped one of the biggest pricks I've seen since Carl, the guard from the Drive in, big eleven inches of manhood.

"Oh my gawd!" what a fucking prick this officer had. He grabbed my head and forced my head down on his cock. I could only manage the head and another few inches in my mouth. He tasted and smelled great.

"Suck my dick, fagot. Lick my balls. Yeah. Lick my dick and balls" He said in an aggressive tone.

"Turn around. I'm gonna fuck your fagot ass. I was watching that man as he fucked his cock up your ass. I'm gonna give your slutty ass a good fucking too. Get on the bed, Bitch, I'm gonna fuck the hell out of you."

I got on the bed as he demanded. Then he got on the bed, still fully clothed, boots and all, lifted my legs and guided his big eleven inch cock to my moist hole. He stuck his thick finger into my moist hole. After he found my entry spot, he rubbed his cock over my hole. He didn't wait for my guidance, but shoved his cock all the way into my asshole. It hurt like hell for a few minutes. He paused for about one minute then started fucking me rough and hard. I was being ravaged by this hunky Security Guard...and I was loving it.

It hurt like hell at first but after a while he began to rub my 'special spot', until it started to feel great.

He had a hot fit body. I unsnapped his shirt and rubbed my hands over his muscular chest and caressed his hairy brown nipples. I could feel his big balls slapping against me. His hat tilted to one side of his handsome face. He was a very handsome and hot looking man. He looked down and me and frowned.

"Tell me how much you like it, fagot. Tell me how my cock feels up your fagot ass. Tell me cocksucker. You like me screwing your boy cunt, don't you?" He said as he roughly manhandled me. He was fierce but I was beginning to like it. He was such a hot stud I would give him my ass anytime. Damn. He was forceful and I liked it.

"Oh yes sir. I love your big cock up my fagot ass. Fuck me Officer Adam. Fuck my fagot ass. Fuck me. Make me your bitch. Fuck my boy-pussy. Oh gawd, your big cock feels so great up my slutty ass. Oh Yeah. Fuck me. Fuck me. Fill me with your manly cum. Breed me."

I kept replying to him as he manhandled me for his pleasure. First it was for his satisfaction to humiliate me but after a few hard shoves I was enjoying it. I liked his demanding ways. Damn. He was driving me crazy. I was gonna cum soon. I was going wild being fucked by this hot rough officer.

The bed was banging against the cabin wall. I was all bent over and finding it hard to breathe. He just kept plunging his thick cock into my abused hole. I could feel his battering ram touching spots that I never knew existed. I was cumming again. He never paused as I came but kept fucking me until he came, and when he started to cum, he shook and let out a deep heavy moan and rammed me harder and harder, spreading my legs like a wishbone. I thought the bed might collapse during his wild fucking.

"Take my load, you fucken fagot slut. Take it cocksucker. Damn it feels so fucken good shooting my sperm up your fagot cunt. Fuck you, you slut. Fuck you bitch. Aww aww, aww. Fuckkkk." He kept talking to me as he came.

"You're one lucky son of a bitch, getting my man seed up your fagot cunt. Oh yeah. You lucky, bitch." Then he paused and rammed into me a few more times. Then he stopped fucking and caught his breath and composed himself. He stared down at me again before pulling his member out of my well used hole.

I could feel his cum leaking from my hole. I just lay there like a despoiled boy-pussy, and it was awesome. He wiped his cock on my leg and on the sheet, then got up, redressed and set back on the bed.

"Are you okay? I have a tendency to get carried away when I get some good ass. You're the first guy I've ever laid. Not bad! Not bad at all. Are you gonna be around this area for a few days? If so perhaps I could call on you again. I've gotta run now. My name's Adam and I have a phone at the lake entrance booth. Here's my card. Give me a call when you have some spare time. Stay cool when you call me. I'm married. Thanks for the good time. See ya later pal."

I really had a good time letting Officer Adam fuck me, even though he was rough. I guess I could manage to let him fuck me again sometime this week-end before we left the lake. I had to pull the sheets off the bed and straighten up before the guys got back from the lake.

I went to the toilet and put some soothing cream around and into my well fucked hole. My hole was sensitive from that last fucking but I heal fast, besides I wanted to keep the guys happy for the next few days.

I slipped into my bathing suit and headed down to the boathouse. The guys had taken the boat out on the lake and were water skiing. I set on the dock and watched the people on the lake.

The Fisherman's Catch

There was a man fishing on the end of the pier. He turned and nodded to me. "How's it going? You don't mind if I fish here do ya?"

"No. I'm sure the owners don't care, besides Roy and the other guys are out in the boat messing around. I'm just a guest. Are you having any luck fishing?"

"Gnaw. I'm giving up for today. Sometimes when it's quiet I catch a few small ones but today the lake is too busy and they scare the fish away." He said as he started pulling his real in and gathering up his gear. He was a good-looking man about 35. Short cut hair, nice body and a pleasant smile.

"Why aren't you out with your buddies on the lake?"

"I've had a rough day and fell asleep, besides I'm not much of a water person. I do most of my playing on dry land. Hi. My names Dick."

"They have a nice boat house here. Do you mind if I go inside and look around, besides I need to take a piss and don't want to stand here on the pier and expose myself. Do you mind?"

"Yeah. Come on. Let's go inside. I've never seen the inside of the boathouse either."

He rested his pole against the side of the boathouse and set his fishing box on the deck and followed me inside. It was just a small area for the boat. A few ores and life jackets hanging around the walls. He move to the edge of the water, pulled down his shorts, and aimed his cock to the water. I thought I'd join him. This way I could get a good look at what he was concealing under his shorts.

"Oh man. Almost nothing better than taking a good piss." He said as a heavy stream of golden piss gushed out of his flaccid cock. Then I added. 'Unless it's a good cocksucker draining the spunk from your cock." He laughed at my addition comment. I couldn't piss because I was starting to get a hard on while watching him piss.

"Yeah. You've got that right. It's been a long time since I've had a good blow job from anyone. How about you?" My cock was uncontrollable and I immediately got a boner. He looked at my hard cock. "Looks like you could use a blow job as well." His piss stopped flowing and he started to get hard. I reached over and caressed his hardening cock.

"Do you want to suck on my cock?" He turned towards me as his shorts fell to his ankles. I leaned over and put his moist cock into my mouth. It started getting hard immediately. I dropped to my knees and took his cock all the way into my mouth. His cock was about eight inches long, once it got hard. I caressed his balls and engulfed his cut cock and ran my tongue around the big tulip shaped head, then when down on him again.

He stood with his hands on his hips and breathed deeply as I pleasure him. He consent to let me pleasure his hard cock for a few minutes before he started producing more and more juices, then he stiffened his body, put his hands on the back of my head, and out gushed several loads of sweet juicy man cum. I sucked it all down and swallowed every precious drop.

His knees buckled as he stood but soon got his composure and gave out a deep sigh of relief.

"Fuck. Young man I really needed that. Damn it was good. I could use a mouth like yours every day. That was a surprise. I never took you as a cock sucker."

I pulled up his shorts and stood as he continued. "I'm here for the next few days staying in my cabin next door to yours. I'm a writer and this place is usually nice a quiet and it gives me time to think and write. My name Conner. Feel free to come over and 'visit' with me again. Now that I am sexually relieved, I'll be able to write some more today." He said as he laughed and put his hand on my shoulder.

"It was my pleasure and if you need to be sexually relieved again I'll come over and give you satisfaction. You have a nice suckable cock. I'll like to visit you sometime soon."

Just then we heard the motor of the boat coming up to the dock. We casually walked outside the boathouse. "See ya soon, friend, and be sure to visit me soon." He said as the boys boat pulled to the dock. Chad threw me the tie line and I secured the boat. Soon the guys were unloading the water skis and other items. We walked up to the cabin to get something to eat. It has been a surprisingly good day for me. I was already looking forward to our evening when we were going to bed. Now that everyone was relaxed around each other our sex would be even better than before.

Evening of Naked Fun and Sex

After we got settled in the cabin, everyone stripped down naked and watched an adult DVD that Roy had brought to watch on the player. The guys didn't need much to get them horny again and I was soon down on the floor between Roy's hard cock sucking out another hot load of cum.

While I was sucking Roy, Chad decided he'd fuck me before Jason got his big dick in me again. This time Chad fucked for a much longer time and every time he was close to cumming, he'd pause and let his cock cool down. He was more relaxed this time until he decided to unload, then he pumped me hard and shot a big load.

Roy came once while Chad was fucking me, but as I continued to drink down his load, he started to get hard again so I kept sucking him. Soon as Chad pulled his soft cock from my asshole, Jason mounted me and eased his big cock deep in my wet slutty hole. I could hear the slushy cum juices from Chad's big load as Jason entered me.

"Dick. I love fucking your wet hole after you've taken my buddies cum. You're so warm and smooth and better than any pussy I've ever fucked. I guess you know you are spoiling us by giving us such good ass without complications. Roy. You sure know how to entertain your guest. You're number one on my list."

Jason fucked me for another ten minutes or so, then he pumped me full of his hot load and laid on my back resting. Meanwhile as Jason came, Roy gave me another load of his nectar. Chad was jacking on his cock, waiting for me to take his next load. These guys knew how to enjoy sex and I was thrilled I was the receptacle of their gifts. Once again I was their pleasure pussy-boy and cum dump…..and I was ecstatic and content.

Ray got up from the couch, turned off the DVD player and went to bed. Jason eased his spent cock from my pussy and lay on the floor. Chad was close by on the couch still jacking on his cock so I crawled to him and started blowing him and took his final load of the evening. He stretched out on the couch and fell asleep. I got up and went to the toilet to deposit the last few loads of cum from my last fucks, cleaned up and crawled into bed with Roy.

During the early morning Roy was guiding his cock into my ass for another fuck. I willingly pushed back against him to let him use me and once again. He came in me and fell asleep. I got up to take a pee and desired I would go outside to get some fresh lake air. I wrapped a towel around my shoulders and set on the back steps in the night air.

Trying Something Kinky

I could hear the sound of frogs, crickets and occasional night owl in the distance. The night air was warm and everything was so quiet and pleasant. I heard the screen door open and turn to see it was Jason. He was still naked and looked so sexy in the light of the full moon.

"Hey Dick. Scoot over. Can I join you? I found a small joint in my bag and thought I'd share it with you. Are you willing?"

"Yeah sure Jason. I've never smoked any before but I am curious. Set here on my towel with me."

Jason set beside me and lit up the joint and took a puff then offered me a smoke. I took a short puff and coughed. He laughed and put his arm around my shoulder, pulled me close and played with my ear.

"You're a swell kid, Dick. How did you become such a sexy thing? I really like you. Are you and Roy a 'thing' or are you just good friends? He talks about you a lot."

"Gnaw. I met him at the Drive-In Theater and we made it together a few times. He's good sex. I like a guy that likes to have sex and cums a lot, and likes to fuck me as well."

"I like to cum a lot too. I hope we can become good friends as well. Here try the grass one more time. Just inhale a small bit and hold it in. That's it, now hold it in, and slowly exhale. You'll feel the results soon."

Jason held me close and kissed me on the cheek. I turned and our lips touched lightly, then he pulled me closer and gave me a deep tongue sucking kiss. I had never been one to kiss much but this was nice. Jason was a handsome dude and his attentions were pleasurable.

"Woo. That was a nice kiss, Dick. I want to take a piss before I get hard again. Say. Would you like to try something kinky?"

"I don't know. What did you have in mind?"

"Have you ever taken a guy's piss? I mean have you swallowed any piss directly from a cock? I've always wanted to do it. I've read it can be very sexual. I was gonna piss in your ass the last time I fucked you, but didn't want to do it without letting you know first. Wanna try it? I won't force you but if you will just put your mouth over my soft dick while I let some piss flow into your mouth….it might be fun?"

"Okay Jason. But be patient with me. I've tasted piss before but never swallowed on purpose."

Jason was already standing and ready to piss. He directed his cock to my mouth and waited for me to take him. I swallowed, and put his cock into my mouth and held onto his big low hanging balls. I waited as Jason pissed a small amount in my mouth. I swallowed the small amount of piss then engulfed his soft cock as he let loose with a larger load. I could feel the warm fluid running down my gullet. I pulled back and started swallowing as his piss flowed into my mouth.

"Gawd Dick. You did it, you did it. I love ya boy. It felt so different. Look at me already. My cock is growing so hard again. Give me one of your fantastic blow jobs, babe. You are sensational. Oh yeah. I love your hot mouth over my cock. Mum, Mum. That is so good. Take your time."

I had taken Jason's piss and it wasn't bad at all. Perhaps next time we can do it better. I continue to work on Jason's big ten inch cock. He held my head and face fucked me then shot another big load into my body along with his warm piss.

After I drained him he slowly set down next to me on the stairs again. He pulled my face to his and started kissing me like before. I liked the way he kissed. My cock was so hard. I started jacking on it but before I could cum, Jason leaned over and took my cock in his mouth. I warned him I was gonna cum, but he kept his mouth over my gushing cock as I came. He continued to suck all my cum and then he swallowed.

I was amazed that his 'straight stud' was sucking on my cock and drinking down my load. It must have been the 'high' from the grass. He took his mouth from my cock and started kissing me again. I could taste my own cum as he kissed me.

"Wow. That was a first for both of us. Huh? Kind of nice. I liked it." Jason said to me as we cuddled on the back stairs. "I'm gonna go back inside and get some sleep. You, coming with me?"

"No. I got a nice nap while you guys were on the lake today. Think I'll set here for a while. Good night Jason. See ya later?"

Jason gave me one more sweet kiss and headed into the cabin. "Oh by the way, Dick, Roy said Carl and Jeff will be coming by in the morning to join us. You know the two security guards from the Theater."

Oh yeah I remember those two hunks with the big cocks, I said to myself. I guess I'll have to give them some time and give them a blow job or perhaps let them both fuck me again.

"Will Roy's dad be joining us too Jason?"

"I don't think so. Why do you ask? How do you know his dad?"

"He dropped by yesterday to see how we all were getting along. I guess I forgot to tell Roy. He only stayed for a short time."

I realized I shouldn't have said anything to Jason about Roy's dad coming by to eat my boy pussy and suck out his own son and his two friends cum after they fucked me. Oh boy. I hope I didn't goof up. I tried to change the subject but decided I'd said enough already.

"Why didn't you tell Roy he dropped by?"

"I don't know. I guess I just forgot about it. He seemed to be a nice man, Jason. Mr. Jordan is a very handsome man. Does he play around?"

"I don't know Dick, but you be cool around him and don't let on about us fucking around this week end."

"Sure Jason. You better get some sleep. I'll be in later. Good night again?"

Jason went inside as I set on the stair steps.

Lap Dance from my Fisherman Friend

As I set on the cabin back stairs, I observed a dark figure on the porch of the cabin next door, and the blinking of a small flashlight. I realized it was the neighbor Conner, the fisherman I sucked off at the boathouse today. He was beckoning for me to come over. I wrapped the towel around my waist and went to his back porch where he was setting naked, in the dark on a lounge chair.

"Hi. Dick. I saw you setting on the stairs and thought perhaps you'd like to join me in conversation. I saw you and your buddy on the stairs but didn't want to disturb you.

My cabin sets higher and I can see directly into your cabin's main room. I saw you sucking your buddies and watched them gang banging your ass. It was very stimulating watching the action. I almost came over to join you."

"You should have joined us, but I'd rather be alone with you. I see your cock is hard and ready for some action. How about a lap dance?" I said as I dropped my beach towel and straddled Conner setting on the lounge chair.

I spread my buttocks and eased myself down on his hard throbbing cock. He looked contented as I set on his cock. I was still wet from Roy's last deposit so it was easy to engulf his cock all the way down to his balls. He didn't protest but let out a grunting sound and a groan of satisfaction.

"Man you are full of surprises. That's a great feeling. You took my whole cock with one movement. Oh man. Oh man. What a sensation. Ease up, or I'll cum right away. I want to enjoy this. My first boy-pussy lap dance. Oh. Yeah." Conner said as he lifted me up and down on his hard eight inch cock. I looked into his handsome face as his cock slid in and out of my wet hole.

He leaned forward to give me a kiss. He had a small mustache. I'd never been kissed by a man with a mustache before. It was nice. He kissed me tenderly while he eased his throbbing cock in and out of my boy-pussy. We fucked for about 10 minutes. I caressed his balls and sensed he was about to have an orgasm. I leaned forward and kissed him while he started cumming.

He went wild moaning and groaning with pleasure as he shot load after load of cum into my hole. He discharged so much cum that it drenched from around his cock and ran down my balls. When he came, I came at the same time and left a wet clammy muddle between our bodies. We continued to kiss for a few minutes as his cock remained semi-rigid in my love tube.

Back to Bed with Roy and Chad

I tried to be quiet as I got back in bed with Roy and discovered Chad was taking a leak in the toilet. I nodded to him and watched him piss. He had a partial hard on. I waited until he finished then went into the toilet with him and gripped his hard cock and run my hands up and down his taunt abs. I leaned over to taste his cock. He sighed and put his hand to the back of my head. He softly said to me.

"Dick. That feels good, but I'd like to fuck you again?. Your boy pussy is so nice and warm."

"I was hoping you'd say that. Let's go to your bed and get more comfortable. Maybe I should clean myself out first. I was just fucked by that hot dude next door and I'm so full of his cum."

"Oh no! I like a wet pussy. Stay just as you are. You are such a slut and that's what turns me on with you. Jason and I fuck this cunt at the college after a few other guys have filled her with cum. She has such a sloppy pussy, and I like it like that. Tell me about the guy next door. How the hell did you get him to fuck you tonight? I know him. He's a literature professor from the college we attend. Fuck. That's hot. Let's go to bed before I cum right here."

Chad and I went into the other room to his bed. He wanted me to lie on my back while he lifted my legs to his shoulder. He quickly guided his prick to my wet and sloppy hole and shoved it in to the hilt. He signed.

"Oh man. You boy pussy is so nice and warm. Feels better that that 'bitch' at college. You're now our bitch. Would you like to be our bitch? I think some of the dudes at the college would like to fuck your sloppy boy pussy sometime. I bet you'd like that, wouldn't you, bitch."

Chad was using me as his 'bitch'. He was getting talkative and liked the idea of making me his 'bitch'. He was a good fucker and we fucked for a long time that night, and when he did cum I came at the same time. He even leaned over and kissed me during our session.

I noticed Jason was watching us from his bed and jacking off at the same time. He shot all over himself while we were fucking. Chad and I fell asleep in each other's arm.

Arrival of Jeff and Carl

I noticed a Jeep pull up outside the cabin and knew it was Carl and Jeff. I continued my breakfast preparations while Roy answered the door to let them in. They brought a case of beer and some groceries to add to the festivities. I hoped they had also brought along a nice load of cum in their balls as well. Even after being fucked at least a dozen times the day before, I was still ready to take on a few more good fuckers. Both Jeff and Carl were hung very well could cum a couple time in an hour. It looked like it was gonna be another day of hot sex. Now I had more men to satisfy at the Lake Cabin.

My first day at the cabin was unbelievable. I had 3 hunky college students using me all day and night, as well as a next door hot College professor, his step son and Roy's father, all using me for their cum dump and love slut. I hadn't forgotten about the Lake Security stud Adam that had dropped by while I was being fucked by Roy's dad. Adam was one of the wildest fuckers I'd ever had and I was looking forward to having him again soon.

I lost track of how many times the college students fuck me, or how many loads of cum I drank that day. I was in cocksucker, ass fuckers' heaven. I was a true unadulterated slut and pussy boy for as many men that wanted to use me for their cum dump slut. It appeared I just couldn't get enough cock, but I was sure willing to try.

Today Jeff and Carl the two security guys from the drive-in had dropped by to have a quick beer with the guys and probably throw a fuck into me before they went to work this evening. Jeff was the one that 'busted my cherry ass' and introduce me to another stimulating way to share my body with other men for pleasure. I was eager to share my natural talent with some of my younger buddies at school, and perhaps the new coach at my high school. I wanted him to fuck me so bad.

We all began our regular routine. Ray and Chad were going to set up the boat for water skiing and fishing, while I cooked up some breakfast for the hungry horny group of studs. I had to feed them well to keep their energy up. I knew my turn would come for them to feed me more cock and cum. I never anticipated these hunks could fuck and cum so much but who was I to complain? I was ready and willing 24 hours a day to service their needs and my hungry mouth and twitching male pussy.

~=*0*=~

Roy, being a good host, introduced Carl and Jeff to his college friends, Chad and Jason and directed them to the back screened-in-porch to get a beer. On the way to the back porch, both Carl and Jeff gave me a hi-five and greeted me like old friends. Carl stepped into the kitchen area to give me a hug from my backside, slid his hand down my shorts to my ass crack, and slipped one of his fingers in my moist hole. His large finger was about the size of some of my high school buddies pricks. He was about a head and a half taller than I, and kissed me on the top of my head as his finger slid all the way in my love canal. He 'finger-fucked' me while he spoke softly in my ear.

"I believe my 'fuck buddy' is ready for some more cock today, huh? Jeff is going to stay here while the rest of us go to the boathouse. He's going to dump a big load up your hot fucken ass so I'll be able to fuck you when I return. We, going to take some quick movies of you and me breeding. I plan to send it to the 'bitch' that dumped me last week for some asshole. I want her to watch and drool over my big cock as I fuck my new 'bitch'. She'll shit when she realizes I'm fucking a 'pussy boy's cunt'. No faces, just cock and ass. I've saved my morning load for your sweet pussy. Got to go now but I'll be back soon. "He slid his finger out of my moist ass and stuck it in my mouth. "I'm so horny. Let me see you lick that," - he said to me. – "Yeah good bitch."

Roy yelled at Carl to hurry up. Jeff stayed behind and came back into the kitchen with a beer. He set the beer on the counter and turned me around facing him. He gave me a nice hug and started kissing me. He pulled down both our trunks and pressed his body into my waiting crotch. His hands firmly cupped my butt cheeks and squeezed.

"I've missed your handsome face and body, but most of all I miss making love to you and fucking your tight boy pussy. Go down on me, swallow my cock and get me hard. I'm gonna throw a fuck into to you right now," he whispered in my ear. I was delighted to suck on Jeff's fat thick cock and lick his balls. He lifted my body and placed my bare buttocks on the counter. He was ready for more bubbling action. My ass was level with his hard dick. Standing on the floor he lifted my legs to his shoulder, licked my ass than guided his cock to my hole and buried it deep in my body.

"Oh Gawd, Dick. Your pussy hole is so warm and tight. I truly love to fuck you more than any hole I'd ever fucked before. Aw yes! Aren't you glad I popped your sweet little cherry hole? I know you love men using your 'fuck hole' to make your men happy: so make me happy. Make me cum in your boy whore pussy." Then Jeff started to fuck his dick in and out of my hole like it was part of me that needed to be completed.

If someone came in the room they'd see me lying backwards on the kitchen island, my legs on my lover's shoulders while this hot stud was shoving his cock in and out of my ass. What a picture this would make. I wasn't exactly comfortable on this hard table, but the feeling of Jeff's cock sliding in and out of my erogenous ass was enough distraction to make me soon forget my discomfort. His cock felt sensational and the feeling of his balls popping against me was erotic. I loved the sound of it and I love how it felt as he plunged away at my hole.

I reached for his neck and pulled myself closer so I could get all of his 8-inch cock deep inside my boy cunt. Gawd! Jeff was a good fucker. I held onto his legs while he squirted my hole full of cum. He was lubrication my ass so his buddy Carl could use me later to fuck the shit out of me with his massive 11-inch cock. Now that is a good friend to have around. Oh yeah, that's a good friend all right. As Jeff filled my hole with his nut juice, he leaned forward and kissed me.

"Babe. You are one hell of a good sport and a damn cool sex partner. I'm sure glad you are so willing to get laid. Most of my female bitches play hard to get after they get their mangy paws on your money. And then when you're hard and ready to pop your load, they have some excuse not to have sex with you. But not you, you're a man's man and a good friend and relief station. Damn I think I love ya."

"I hear the guys coming back from the tour of the boat house. Thanks again for being my cum dump for now. I'm not leaving for work today without fucking you again or getting one of your nut busting blow jobs. I hope you're lubed enough to take Carl's horse cock. He's hot for your hole. Now give me a quick kiss and I'll get you off that table. Get on your knees and lick the extra juices from my dick. – I want you to clean me good"

Jeff lifted me from the counter and set my feet back on the floor. I faithfully dropped to my knees and licked his dick and balls clean. Just as I stood, the guys were coming up the porch stairs. We had finished just in time.

"I hope you two have gotten acquainted again and lubed his sweet ass for me." Carl said as he entered the room. "I told the guys what I wanted to do to get even with that last bitch I was dating. Dick. If you're ready to help me out, go to the bed area and we'll set up the camera. Like I said before, no faces, just dick, balls and asshole. Come on guys, you all can watch but no talking in case someone recognizes your voice. You can watch only until we finish fucking. I want this to be good enough so we can upload it to U-Tube."

Setting up for a Movie

I went into the bedroom and pulled the top covers off the bed. Meanwhile Roy was setting up a movie camera at the foot of the bed. Jeff had brought his laptop PC with a build in camera to record and to get another angel. I put some baby oil all over my body, especially my buttocks, so they would stand out in the film. Everything was ready.

I was instructed to suck Carl's big cock and get him hard. I was to lie on my back and wait for him to get on the bed, between my legs and rub his cock head against my butt. He would proceed to impale his large cock into my ass. The camera was to start just as he stroked his cock and lubed it with oil getting it ready to penetrate me.

First he was to lift my legs to shoulders and feel my ass. Then he was to slowly spread my cheeks apart and finger my hole. Next Carl would ease his dick into me until it was out of sight. Then everything that followed would become natural for a guy on guy fuck scene.

I had been fucked by Carl in that position once before. It seemed comfortable for both of us. I liked it this way because I could watch his face as he pleasured himself in my love canal. I usually came while Carl fucked me because his cock always rubbed the right spot at the right time. My hole became so full of his cock, that it felt extraordinary.

I was so into getting fucked by Carl, I almost forgot we were being filmed. I trusted the guys not to show our faces at any time. It was mainly for Carl's benefit. He was going to send the part where his cock was going in and out of my ass. He was going to dump, and then slowly pull his cock out of my hole to show her he had cum in my pussy boy's hole. And it was manly good. If a guy can take his cock and satisfy him, why couldn't she do the same? He wanted to make her jealous and he was sure this would do it.

Carl got into position, lifted my legs and rubbed his cock up and down my ass crack. He inserted two fingers into the opening of my moist hole. I was hoping none of Jeff's cum was still oozing out of my ass. Carl pulled his finger out of my hole, lifted my legs even higher and slowly placed the head of his cock to my opening. I spread my butt cheeks encouraging his entry. He eased in slowly. We both sighed and I shuttered. No matter how many times a cock enters me it makes me feel sensational. It's hard to describe. Most of the time I tremble. Carl's big cock made me feel so good.

He paused long enough to let the camera get a 'close up' of his cock going into my asshole. Then he really started to fuck me. First it was slow and easy, then as he fucked he build up a rhythm and started pounding me fast and furious. I could feel his crescendo coming any minute. His dick swelled in my love track. That always caused me to cum. I gasp and grabbed his buttocks to pull him deeper into my welcome body. I wanted him inside me. I really didn't want this fuck to end but then he cut loose and moaned out a deep guttural sound of sexual pleasure "Oh Fuck. I'm Cumming in your tight boy pussy. You are the best. Aw yes. Cumming, deep in your boy cunt. You are the best fuck ever. Aw fuck!"

When he came. I could feel the warm gush of man juices being emptied deep inside my body. I was cumming at the same time causing my ass muscles to tighten. That always cause my partner to enjoy the tight grip around his cock muscle. Eventually he pulled out and collapsed to lie beside me.

We lay together for a short time as the camera came closer to watch my cum filled ass release Carl's sperm and man juices from my hole. After a short while, someone said 'cut', and everyone applauded. I was so relaxed from the good fucking that I almost fell asleep. I looked up to see all of the guys standing around the bed jacking on their cock.

"Let's have a circle jerk." someone suggested. "Let's get closer to Dick and jack off all over his body and face."

"Oh Yeah. That sounds like a great idea." I said

"I want your milk guys, I want cum to fill my mouth and drench my body. I am your cum dump. Cum on me please. Give me your manly nectar; the sweet body nectar of the gods; feed me and make me immortal with your love juices." – I said to them.

I'd often dreamed of guys standing over me and covering me with cum. This was the one chance to have my dream come true. The four hunky guys stood on the bed and directed their cocks to my body. In almost perfect unison they shot big loads on my face, in my mouth, and all over my body. Whatever I couldn't get in my mouth dripped on to my chest and stomach. I gulped, swallowed and licked the fingers of my users. I loved every minute, every gob and every sticky flavor that dropped from their cocks. I was drenched with the nectar of these gods. Don't kid yourself guys – If you work at it and follow your dreams; they sure as hell do come true.

The End

Here is a sample from another story you may enjoy:

Dick Clinton

COMMUNITY SERVICE

Hot Gay Erotica

One of my distant cousins passed on and left me a small cabin and five acres of land near a small town called Lake View on the 'Lake of the Ozarks'. The cabin was located just outside the city limits near a fairly busy state highway exit. I'd only met my cousin one time at a family meeting in Springfield, Missouri when my grandfather was ill. We seemed to bond together at our first meeting. I had a special 'Gay-dar' feeling about him and I assumed he felt the same towards me. But why in the hell did he leave me this cabin?

I had some long merited vacation coming, so I thought I would go to the Lake to check it out. I was living in Kansas City at the time and the property was only a few hours by car. I left early in the morning so it would still be light when I arrived. I only stopped once to eat at a truck stop, fill up my gas tank, and check out the area for future cruising.

When I arrived at the Lake it was still light so with the directions the attorney gave me, I had no problem finding it. It was a small log cabin cottage nestled among some pine trees. I was surprised how nice and cozy it looked. One thing that puzzled me was the large empty field at the side of the property that seemed to be used for parking large trucks. I wasn't sure if my cousin Peter was a truck driver or not, but there seemed to be plenty of room to park two or three trucks.

I went inside the cabin to explore the layout. It had a nice entrance to a living room and hallway. A large stone fireplace was centered in the west wall. At the other side of the room was a small eating area directly next to an open kitchen, which was a little out of date, but it had an average size stove with oven and a nice refrigerator and a microwave oven. The place was well stocked with dishes, pans, flatware and other utensils. The oven and fridge were clean as well as the remainder of the room. There was a door at the back of the Kitchen which I would explore later.

I went back to the hallway that directed me to one small bathroom and two small bedrooms. The cabin was fully furnished and very neat and clean. I was surprised that someone hadn't broken in and stolen anything, but the place had been left intact. I didn't notice a TV so I would have to find out about that later.

While I was exploring the cabin I was startled to hear the sound of my telephone ringing. I went to the kitchen to answer the old fashioned, wall-hanging phone. When I picked up the phone to speak I was surprised to hear a woman's voice.

"Hello. Is this Clint?"

"Yes," I quickly said.

"This is Mildred at the phone company. Your attorney called me yesterday and said you were coming. We have connected your phone and I had my brother Walter come over yesterday to make sure your propane gas tank was full and working properly. My daughter and niece came by yesterday to clean your house and put on fresh bedding on both beds and clean towels and more linens in the hallway closet.

"We saw you come through town today. My brother will be out to show you things about your gas tank, and how to get the water pump going so you'll have some water for your cabin. We've turned the electricity on so you should be pretty well situated.

"Sorry about losing your cousin," Mildred went on. "Peter was a good man and will be missed around here. If you have any more questions about the cabin, I'm sure Walter can help you out there. I also own the grocery store so if you need supplies all you have to do is call me. I'll fill out your grocery list and have Bobby bring it out tonight. Your attorney has taken care of most of the expenses so once again welcome to Lake Shore. You'll find a list of phone numbers in the top drawer of the counter.

"Now have a good day and I'll be expecting your call for the groceries or any other supplies you might need. Got to go now. The mail has arrived and I have to separate the mail for tomorrow's delivery. You all be good now. Bye."

Before I could say anything she hung up. I think she said all that in one breath. What a talker, but now I'm sure I will be well taken care of here. I headed out to get my suitcases, some clothes, and a few boxes of things I thought I might need at the cabin. Just as I was opening the trunk of the car, along came a pick-up truck. It was probably Walter.

"Howdy, neighbor. I take it you're Clint. I'm Walter.

"Here, let me carry some of that stuff for you, buddy. I trust you had a good trip from KC. I came by yesterday to set up and fill your propane tanks. I didn't turn on your water pump yet cause I wanted to show you how to do it. You have a well house out back that pumps water from your well and into your cabin. Your septic tank is down the hill there and was drained last month. I gather my sister Mildred called you about most everything else. Nice to have someone living here again. All us men will miss Peter a lot. He was a great friend and a fantastic cock sucker."

We were in the cabin when he said "Peter was a fantastic cock sucker." I almost dropped the suitcases when he said that. I assumed at first it was just a 'man thing' a person says about another man in casual conversation.

Walter saw my shock, then he said, "Oh my gawd, Clint. I thought you knew about Peter, since you being a relative and all. Sorry if I shocked you. Why don't you put away some of your things while I pour us a drink and I'll tell you all about good ole Peter?"

I was shocked...in a way. I knew I felt a close connection when I first met Peter, now I knew why. He was gay and somehow he knew I was also. I quickly sat down on the couch while Walter found some liquor and poured us both a drink.

"Here, Clint. Have a drink while I tell you about Peter.

"Peter was a Missouri Highway Patrolman for many years. He lived here before, and even after he retired. He 'entertained' many truckers and biker friends that he met over a period of time, and I might add many of the locals, visiting fishermen, and hunters that came down during the seasons. And yeah, I said the 'locals' as well.

"We have a certain close knit buddy system here amongst us men. You might say it is like the military, 'don't ask, don't tell.' Most all of the local men would come by to see Peter on a regular schedule for 'man sex.' Our wives didn't know, or if they did know they never let on. I think some of our women folk had suspicions about Peter, but were never told the whole truth. I think they were glad we would visit Peter for sexual relief.

"Peter was like our local whore. The women never complained or said anything about Peter. If they knew he was gay they figured he wasn't gonna take away their men folk because he was a man and not a woman with a pussy. Little did they know Peter's ass was some of the best 'pussy' in town and had the most talented mouth that we used as our cum dump."

"How did Peter die?" I ask.

"I'm not quite sure, but I was told by one of the bikers that works in town, that when there was a 'biker run' through this part of Missouri, they would always make Peter's place one of their yearly stops. He told me Peter volunteered to take on as many men that wanted to use his man pussy for fucking. There were over 25 men here for the party and most of them fucked him at least one time. The next day Peter had a heart attack while sucking off another dozen men. Bless his soul, he died the way he wanted, full of man sperm. He had one of the biggest funerals in this part of the state and was attended by hundreds of men from all around the state. They even had a biker escort to the lake where his ashes were thrown in. It was awesome. "

I sat there dumbfounded, and took another drink of whiskey.

"I hope you aren't upset by me telling you this."

I just sat there in a stupor as Walter continued to talk. After which I answered, "'Nah.   Glad you told me. I have so much to understand about his gay lifestyle."

"Don't forget to call Mildred to get your food order. I should go and let you ponder this."

"Yeah. I'm okay with this, just shocked that everyone knew about Peter except me. Thanks Walter for setting up the gas and water stations for me. I don't have much money on me to give you for your service until I go to the ATM tomorrow. If there's anything that I can do for you, just let me know. Okay?"

He hesitated for a few seconds then smiled and tugged on his cock through his pants.

"Now don't take offense, you're a nice looking young man, and not that you look gay. But I was hoping since Peter left you this cabin, that you might....you know...take over where he left off. There are a lot of good looking, well-hung men that would be so grateful for your continued service....and, well... I could sure use a good blow job before I leave today…"

If you enjoyed this sample then look for **Community Service**.

Also by this Author:

<u>Hard Pounders in Tight Quarters</u>

<u>Safekeeping</u>

<u>Pleasant Encounters and Adventures of Corey</u>

<u>Cop Sucker</u>

<u>The Beach House</u>

<u>Butch Trade</u>

About the Author

I was born in our family home in 1935, after the depression and before WWII, in a small township called Shawnee, Kansas.

After College I joined the US Navy for 4 years. Soon after I was honorably discharged from the navy I met my first gay male companion and lived with him for four more years in Kansas. During that time I worked as an Accountant and part time Professional Male Model for a commercial photo studio for Sears, JC Penny, Goodyear Tire and Tasty Milk Company.

I was offered a job at Denver Business College and worked as an assistant for two more years. During my spare time I attended Barber and Cosmetology Academy and received my state license. I achieved first place as top Stylist of my class, and received a two weeks paid scholarship to Hollywood Beauty College in CA.

After my Hollywood experience I went to Scottsdale, AZ and worked as a style director at Sacs Fifth Ave Salon, until I became allergic to the chemicals I was using and had to resign.

I became active politically in San Francisco and in Metropolitan Community Church of SF and was ordained as Head Deacon for life by Elder Rev. Troy Perry of Los Angeles, CA and can legally marry, perform Baptism and give Holy Communion in the state of California.

I lived, worked, and played in the SF Bay Area until I retired in January 2000 and moved to Surprise, Arizona. I began writing erotic stories after I moved to Arizona. My stories have been published in Handjobs Magazine and by other Blogs on the Internet.

I now live in a home on a senior area of Arizona where I write and enjoy the warm weather of the Arizona sun.

Check my page on Amazon for Updates and interesting info.

Author Central Page - http://amzn.to/1aGgEt5

If you enjoyed any of my books then please share the love and click like on my books in Amazon.

If you write me a review and send me an email I will send you a free book, or many.
(Just know that these emails are filtered by my publisher.)

Good news is always welcome.

One Last Thing, For Kindle Readers...

When you turn the page, Kindle will give you the opportunity to rate this book and share your thoughts on Facebook and Twitter. If you enjoyed my writings, would you please take a few seconds to let your friends know about it? Because... when they enjoy they will be grateful to you and so will I.

Thank You!

Dick Clinton
dick_clinton@awesomeauthors.org

Printed in the USA
CPSIA information can be obtained
at www.ICGtesting.com
LVHW020013190324
774822LV00034B/350